To

OLIVIA,

Love from

Granny &
Granpa
xx.

We love you sweet Olivia,
We love to watch you gr**ow**.

Each day you bring us far more joy
Than you could ever know.

Olivia

Mister
Mouse

We love your morning cuddles,
When you snuggle in so tight.

To see your little dimples
As you laugh at what we've said.

We love you when you try your best
To do something we ask.

To see you try to please us
And complete a tricky task.

We love those little games you play,
That have no rules at all.

Even if eventually
They drive us up the wall!

We love it when you copy us,
And make out like you're baking.

We love you even when you're naughty.
Yes, that's really true!

We love that look of joy when
You get bubbles in your hair.

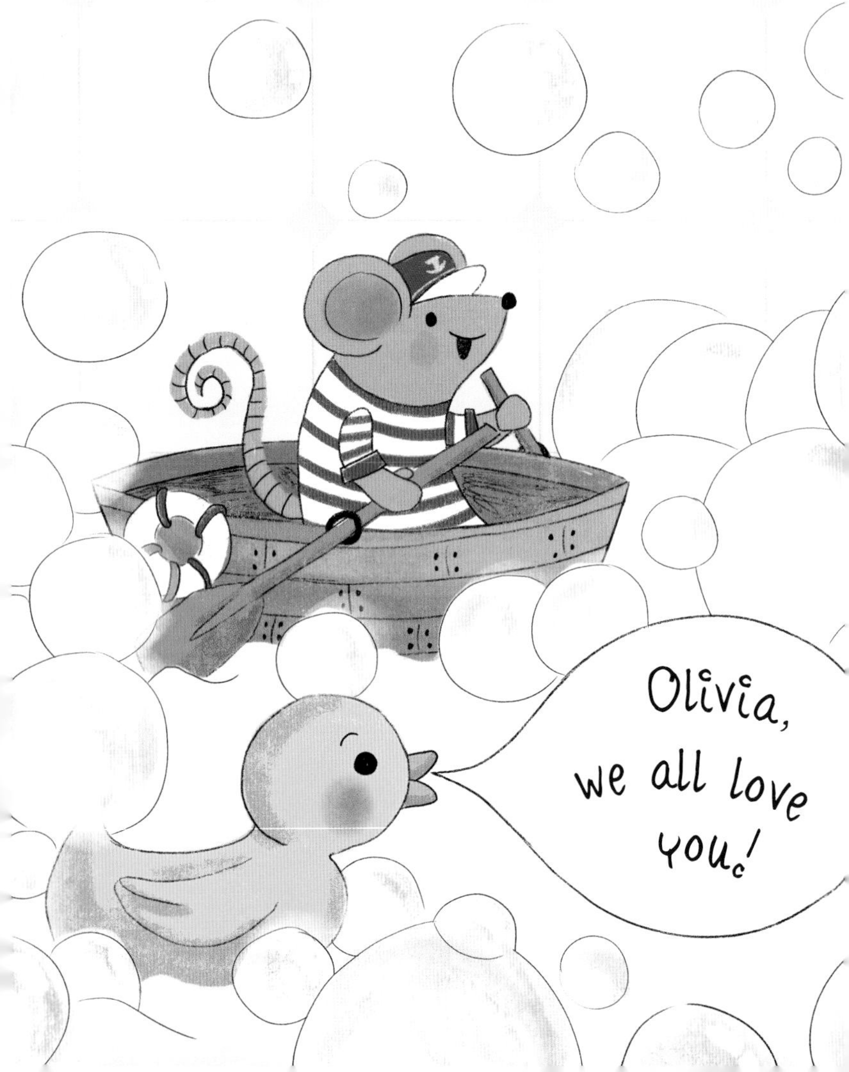

Even when you're splashing
Soapy water everywhere!

We love you when you're feeling angry,
And when you're upset.

We love your little sleepy face
When you cannot stop yawning.

We cannot wait to see you smile
Again tomorrow morning.

Olivia,
we all
love you!

We love the silly things you say,
And funny things you do.

But most of all, Olivia, we love you
For being **YOU!**

OLIVIA,
here are 10 things
we all love about
YOU!

Written by J.D. Green
Illustrated by MacKenzie Haley
Designed by Nicky Scott

First published by HOMETOWN WORLD in 2019
Hometown World Ltd
1 Queen Street
Bath
BA1 1HE

Visit www.hometownworld.co.uk

Follow us @hometownworldbooks

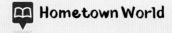